The Imaginary Smile

A Book on Poems

Sourav Dey

CONTENTS

Life

.

I saw a hope, to make some
good,

And four steps were all it took.

The first was trust, but knew
not on whom,

So, I sought to truth, but it got
me the broom.

I thought maybe, that love was
lost,

But no, it actually came at a
cost.

So, kindness was all that I had
left,

Alone and sunken in my quest.

What I learnt was very easy,

In a world of fools,

These thoughts were silly.

The Horizon

.

I looked at the distant, the
beautiful sea,

And saw a horizon, so calm
and glee.

A ship on the edge, drifting
afar,

Saw as I sat, puffing on my
cigar.

Strange how time files and
runs,

Yet the things that were meant
are never done.

A place were freedom and
happiness are free,

But friendship is costly and
my love parted with me.

The horizon gave me hope, of
a beautiful tomorrow,

So today I lived, as if time I
borrowed.

But in this life, I can't deny,

The horizon is the place where
I would like to fly.

Food

I ran over here, and I ran over
there,

Searching for food, to make it
a square.

Two bread and water, was all
for lunch,

As I saw people, waste food
over brunch.

Strange how the rich, gets
options to eat,

Yet we the poor, suffer alone
on the street.

How hunger kills many, but
spares the rich,

How poor children dies, yet
the rich kids live.

Their food is better, its tasty
and warm,

We get the rotten, served with
worms.

If you could spare some food a
day,

Waste a little, and make
someone's day,

You won't be rich, neither
poor,

But a man on the street, would
be happy and more.

Home

I travelled the sea, and the land
afar,

To find a place, under the star.

A place called home, I wanted
to be,

But an act called life,
happened with me.

The closer I wanted, to come
to home,

The further it drove me, away
and alone.

I wished for it, but I was
young,

I thought my parents were
crazy and were no fun.

Finally, when I came back,
with nothing but me,

I cried and cried as I could
finally see.

My home is where my heart
lied, and it was here,

With my parents under a roof
who never stopped to care.

<u>Cure</u>

.

If cure was as easy as the
disease would be,

The pain and the suffering we
would not see.

But God has plans that you
can't deny,

You can't skip or just go by.

It may hurt or it might heal,

But He will never ever reveal.

For sure in this life you find
out why,

God made you happy, or did
He make you cry.

The House

.

Amidst all hardships and
storms, we stood,

And built this house with all
we could.

A nail here and a brick over
there,

Our shoes and cloths suffered
wear and tear,

We smiled through our
problems,

As if we didn't care,

And built this house with all
that was there.

In the end a house, sure was
built,

But without our friends it
couldn't have been fulfilled.

Death

One thing in life that I saw,

Death is fairly a common law.

Be it rich or be it the poor,

Death to all is for sure.

Deeds you may do,

To trade your life,

Some good, some bad and
some other sacrifice.

Lighting a candle or praying to
God,

Will surely not take away the
sins you caused.

Remember the law,

That governs your life.

The reward you will get but
not in afterlife,

For the sin you have done,

You will be punished fair and
square,

For death will guide you and
give you your share.

So be it day or be it night,

Do a deed that makes things
right.

It might be small it might be
big,

Don't hope for results, or you
will fall in the pit,

Throw your greed, throw your
hate,

And in the end, you'll reach
heaven's gate.

<u>Nature</u>

I saw the world, a place so
green,

With people doing good, and
not being so mean.

The tree that provided shade to
many,

Was cut down to earn a few
pennies.

The forest that homes the
mighty king,

Were animals were free, and
birds could sing.

Were burnt to ashes and
cleared away,

To make houses for the stray.

And in the name of defense
you kill,

But those poor animals, just
wanted a meal.

Confused and weak nowhere
to go,

One by one they die by our
blow.

Nature sure keeps a record of
these,

All the actions will bring us to
our knees.

The one who gives, can also
take,

So be careful, for the blow will
ache.

The Banyan Tree

Oh great, astute, powerful and
leafy,

You shelter the poor, and help
the needy.

Your size so huge, yet no
grudge you hold.

You also give wood, to keep
away the cold.

Home you are to so many
birds,

Giving them foods which no
one serves.

For selfish reasons we cut you
in half,

Yet your life you give, away
with a laugh.

You think not of yourself
when help is required,

You throw in your life as if no
greatness you acquired.

If only we could be as half as
great as you,

This Earth our home would be
good as new.

The Rich & The Poor

There was this bridge and it
needed a toll,

To join children with their
dreams and goal.

The rich made it through and
the poor were left,

In need of food, they took to
theft.

The places for the all were
filled up by rich,

And parents felt proud, instead
of filling the breach.

To us, as a human, it's a great
shame,

To force the children to play
this rich and poor game.

A Child's View

I look at the sky, and then at
the sea.

Father and mother, where can
you be.

I searched for you my entire
life.

But it seems you both like to
hide.

My friends at school they beat
me and taunt.

Others come in new dress,
cycle and flaunt.

Why does grown-up say you
live in the stars?

Isn't that place a bit too far?

If you feel cold hold my
hands.

We will talk and walk in this
very land.

I wait for the day when you
will come.

It's already a long time hope I
don't get benumb.

<u>A God</u>

.

To this dark and cruel world, I
want to say,

To make me a man, she kept
her tears at bay.

I saw the woman from my
birth,

And I could never be of her
worth.

She embraced me whenever I
cried,

Oh, mother believe me I really
tried.

She trusts me more than I can,

She said son just be a good
man.

I tried to find God in lands and
seas,

But all my life she was
standing right in front of me.

<u>The Fish</u>

The river that flows, and
mixes with the sea,

Isn't it something beautiful, a
moment of glee?

The sound of water going
down the stream,

Homes the fishes that loves to
swim.

Yet here we are, to throw a
can,

A newspaper, a bottle, all
things that are banned.

Down the river, with the
streams,

Killing the fishes and all their
dreams.

Do you know what it feels?

To not have a mouth?

To go through the dry
summer,

Fighting drought?

It not our fault, still we adjust,

Yet you people are keen to
turn us to dust.

If you can't stop a fight, then
don't start a war,

If you can't heal a wound, then
don't make it more.

<u>The Child</u>

I looked for you in the sky and
sea,

And then I wondered where
you could be?

Is it the stars, or behind the
tree?

Where do you hide and run
from me?

Am I bad, or am I ugly?

That people run away and
nobody loves me.

A friend I want and nothing
more,

To share my troubles and the
sadness I bore.

Don't throw this poem it's my
cry for help,

For all I am is a helpless
whelp.

The Dog

.

Did you ever feel lonely under
the sky?

No food, no shelter, no place
to hide.

A big heart, but nothing to say,

Stones pelt at, by people at
bay.

Come thunder, come rain,

Come cold, come pain,

You have a home and love you
gain.

I get the frames in media and
web,

Likes and comment posed like
celebs.

Once you are done, I am as
good as dead,

I roam the nights as you go to
bed.

Love I will, like the day we
met,

Yet you forget, but do not fret.

Cause my love is not bound by
money,

Or frames or fame because I
don't care for any.

All I want is a friend to see,

In this world who would be
proud of me.